AF228603

CRISIS IN UKRAINE

WAR IN UKRAINE

Tamara L. Britton

Abdo & Daughters
MIDDLE GRADE NONFICTION
An imprint of Abdo Publishing
abdobooks.com

ABDOBOOKS.COM

Published by Abdo Publishing, a division of ABDO, PO Box 398166, Minneapolis, Minnesota 55439. Copyright © 2023 by Abdo Consulting Group, Inc. International copyrights reserved in all countries. No part of this book may be reproduced in any form without written permission from the publisher. Abdo & Daughters™ is a trademark and logo of Abdo Publishing.

Printed in the United States of America, North Mankato, Minnesota.

052022

092022

Editor: Tyler Gieseke

Series Designers: Laura Graphenteen and Colleen McLaren

Cover Photographs: aarows/Alamy Stock Photo (foreground top); DIMITAR DILKOFF/ Contributor/Getty Images/(foreground left), San Francisco Chronicle/Hearst Newspapers via Getty Images/Contributor (background left); Sputnik via AP (background right); Shutterstock Images

Interior Photographs: ALEXANDER KHUDOTEPLY/ Stringe /Getty Images p. 21; Alexander Koerner/ Contributor/Getty Images p. 17; ALEXEY NIKOLSKY/ Contributor/Getty Images pp. 24-25; Anadolu Agency/Contributor/Getty Images pp. 7, 16, 23, 28-29, 33, 59; ANATOLY SAPRONENKO/Staff/AP Images p. 13; ANDREY BORODULIN/Contributor/Getty Images pp. 46-47; ASSOCIATED PRESS/AP Images pp. 52-53, 56-57; Bloomberg/Contributor/Getty Images p. 58; BULENT KILIC/Contributor/Getty Images pp. 38-39; Chris McGrath/Staff/Getty Images pp. 40-41, 49; Heritage Images/Contributor/Getty Images p. 11; THYS/Contributor/Getty Images pp. 34-35; Konstantin Zavrazhin/Contributor/Getty Images p. 32; Kramatorsk_railway_ bombing_2022_April_8_(6) / Wikimedia Commons p. 50; Marcus Yam/Contributor/Getty Images p. 43; National Archives and Records Administration p. 12; NurPhoto/Contributor/ Getty Images p. 44; Pierre Crom/Contributor/Getty Images p. 22; Shutterstock Images 8-9, 18-19, 20, 27, 37, 51, 61; Sipa USA via AP/AP Images pp. 30-31, 42; SPTNK/AP Images p. 55; Sputnik via AP/AP Images pp. 4-5, 6; Stefano Guidi/Contributor/Getty Images p. 45

Design Elements: Shutterstock Images

LIBRARY OF CONGRESS CONTROL NUMBER: 2022934963

PUBLISHER'S CATALOGING-IN-PUBLICATION DATA

Names: Britton, Tamara L., author.

Title: War in Ukraine / by Tamara L. Britton

Description: Minneapolis, Minnesota : ABDO Publishing, 2023 | Series: Crisis in Ukraine | Includes online resources and index.

Identifiers: ISBN 9781532199158 (lib. bdg.) | ISBN 9781098273132 (ebook)

Subjects: LCSH: Ukraine--Foreign relations--Juvenile literature. | Russia (Federation)--Foreign relations--Juvenile literature. | War--Causes--Juvenile literature. | Political and social views-- Juvenile literature.

Classification: DDC 947.708--dc23

TABLE OF CONTENTS

Russian soldiers gathered in Crimea, preparing for the Russian invasion.

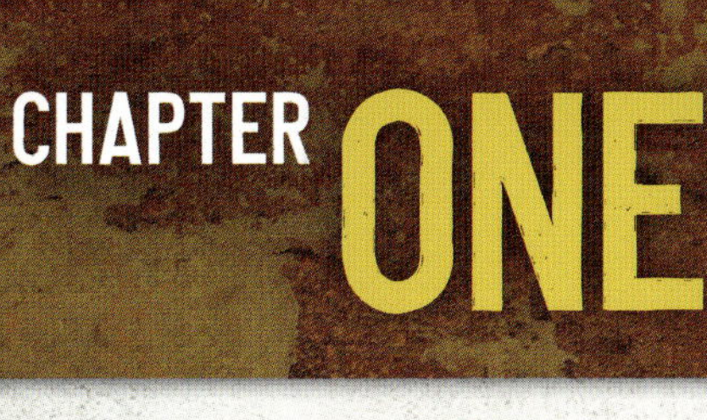

CHAPTER ONE

A HISTORY OF CONFLICT

In February of 2022, the United States (US) and allied governments warned of a possible Russian invasion of Ukraine. Satellite images showed a substantial amount of Russian military hardware and armed forces gathered along the country's border with Ukraine.

There were other events that made officials suspicious. Russia and Belarus had recently carried out joint military exercises called Union Resolve 22. Russia carried out exercises of its GROM nuclear triad, overseen by Russian Federation president Vladimir Putin and president of Belarus Alexander Lukashenko.

Tensions were heightened when, on February 21, Putin recognized the Donetsk People's Republic and the Luhansk People's Republic, known together as the Donbas, as

Russian military vehicles often were marked with the letter Z. This would become a symbol of support for the invasion.

independent states. These breakaway republics had been in conflict with Ukrainian forces since declaring themselves separate from Ukraine after the Revolution of Dignity in 2014.

On February 24, Putin gave a televised speech. In it, he said that for eight years, the Russians had been working to settle the situation in the Donbas peacefully. He said that a coup had occurred against Ukraine's government in 2014. He went on to criticize the United States and the North Atlantic Treaty Organization (NATO), calling them out for waging destructive wars. He said Ukraine joining NATO was unacceptable.

To support the independence of the Donetsk People's Republic and the Luhansk People's Republic, and to stop the bombardment of their cities by Ukrainian forces, Putin announced a special military operation. Within minutes, Russia invaded Ukraine.

The international response was without precedent. World leaders moved to enact the strongest economic sanctions in history. Countries sent millions of dollars and tons of military equipment to help Ukraine defend itself. Ukraine's neighbors welcomed millions of refugees into their countries and supplied shelter, food, medical care, and other necessary assistance.

The fighting was fierce with major losses on both sides. Officials suggested it could last for years. How did Russia and Ukraine—two nations with a long, shared history and culture—get to this point? As with all wars, there were many factors. One was the two countries' experience as members of the Union of Soviet Socialist Republics (USSR).

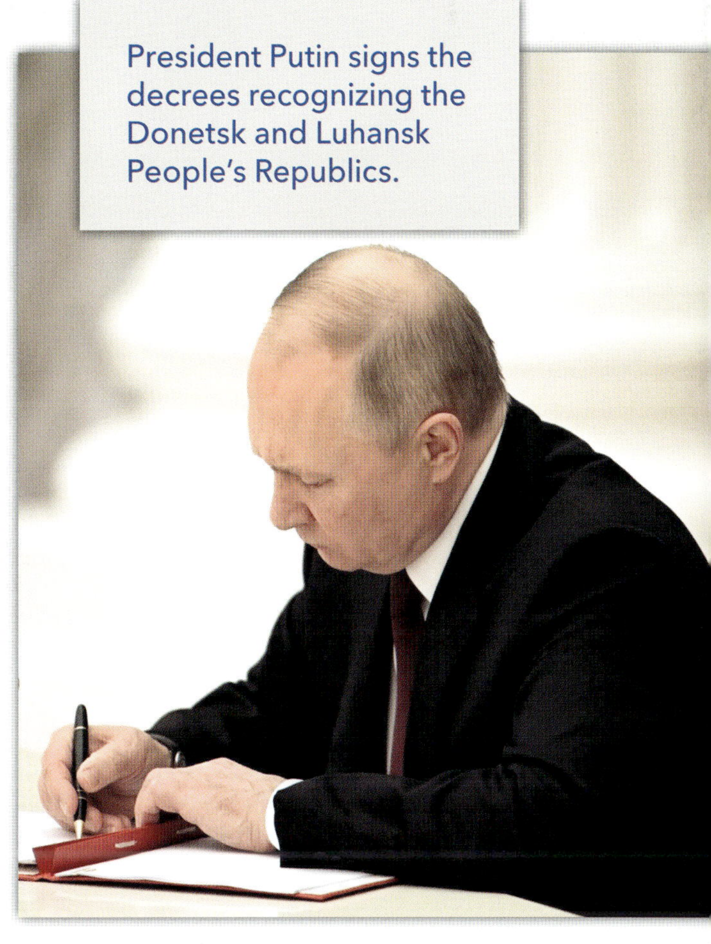

President Putin signs the decrees recognizing the Donetsk and Luhansk People's Republics.

The USSR's government met at the Grand Kremlin Palace in Moscow. Today, it is the official residence of the president of the Russian Federation.

CHAPTER TWO

UKRAINE AND THE USSR

The Union of Soviet Socialist Republics was formed by Vladimir Lenin in 1922. It covered 8.6 million square miles of Europe and Asia. It was made of 15 parts called Soviet Socialist Republics. One of these was the Ukrainian Soviet Socialist Republic.

The USSR was the first country to have a communist form of government. In a communist society, the means of economic production such as factories, farms, and mines are owned by the government. The government distributes goods to individuals according to their needs.

The Soviet government controlled all of the country's land and industry. The country's large landmass made it rich in minerals, petroleum, natural gas, metals, and fertilizer. With these resources, industry thrived.

The USSR's agricultural industry was based on large, state-run farms. Its main crops were grains, potatoes, sugar beets, and vegetables. The harsh climate and short growing seasons made agriculture difficult.

The Ukrainian Soviet Socialist Republic was a major agricultural area. In 1929, Soviet leader Joseph Stalin forced collectivization of farming. Farmers had to give up their land and homes and were forced to farm and live in collectives. This, in addition to the challenges of the climate, caused Soviet farmers to produce less food. These food shortages led to famine.

Some Ukrainian farmers were not happy with collective farming and rebelled against it. Soviet officials responded by not distributing food to Ukraine. Ukrainians were not allowed to leave the Ukrainian Republic to get food.

The Ukrainian peoples' plight increased when Soviet officials confiscated the food they had in their homes. From 1932 to 1933 almost four million Ukrainians perished in a famine called the Holodomor. Soviet officials forbade anyone from speaking of the famine. The immense loss of life would not be acknowledged by the USSR for more than 50 years. But the event is significant in Ukrainian cultural memory.

World War II began on September 1, 1939, when Germany invaded Poland. The previous month Stalin and German chancellor Adolf Hitler signed a nonaggression agreement. However, this did not stop German forces from invading the USSR on June 22, 1941.

Workers on a collective farm near Kyiv, Ukraine. The farm was called a kolkhoz. The workers were kolkhozniks.

Ukraine was one of the republics along the front line. The Germans were ruthless in their advance, taking soldiers as prisoners and killing civilians. But the Soviet forces fought hard to protect their country and to liberate others. They ultimately defeated the Germans in what they call the Great Patriotic War. But the USSR lost an estimated 20 million lives. Five to seven million of those were Ukrainians.

USSR ambassador Andrei Gromyko *(seated)* signed the United Nations Charter on June 26, 1945.

In the years after the war, the USSR had one of the world's largest economies. It had a strong military and was a powerful political force in the world. It was one of the first members of the United Nations (UN). The country developed nuclear weapons in 1949 and eight years later sent the first satellite into space.

But the country had set up communist governments in many countries in Eastern Europe. At the time, the US was another powerful country. It did not want communism to spread. To defend against this, the US and 11 other nations formed NATO in 1949.

In response, the USSR and seven Eastern European nations created the Warsaw Pact in 1955. This standoff led to the Cold War.

During the Cold War, the US and the USSR each tried to expand its own power while working to keep the other from becoming more powerful. The Cold War continued for the next three decades. Then in 1985, Soviet leader Mikhail Gorbachev allowed for more freedom of speech and open elections. But leaders in some republics did not believe these reforms went far enough. They wanted more independence.

On September 5, 1991, Soviet officials met to discuss the future of the country. Over the next months, many republics were granted independence. Ukraine had declared its independence on August 24. On December 1, Ukrainians voted for independence from the USSR. By the end of the year, the USSR had dissolved.

Ukrainians celebrate their independence on August 25, 1991.

The first president of Ukraine, Leonid Kravchuk, previously held several positions in the Ukrainian Soviet Socialist Republic's government.

CHAPTER THREE

INDEPENDENT UKRAINE

Free of Soviet control, on June 28, 1996, Ukraine adopted a new constitution. It granted its citizens the right to own private property. It created the office of the president, who would serve a five-year term and could be re-elected to a second term. It also created a single-house legislature called the Supreme Council of Ukraine. Its members would serve five-year terms. On December 1, 1999, Leonid Kravchuk became Ukraine's first democratically elected president.

But Ukrainians faced many hardships. During the Soviet period, rapid industrialization, intensive farming, and pollution had degraded Ukraine's environment. The country's economy struggled with high inflation and slow growth.

Ukrainians began to look toward a closer relationship with Europe to improve their economy and living standards. However, in 2013, Ukraine's president, Viktor Yanukovych, announced he would not sign the Ukraine-EU Association Agreement that would have begun political and economic relations between the two. Instead, he worked to strengthen ties with Russia.

On November 21, Ukrainians took to the streets to protest government corruption, the influence of oligarchs in government business, and human rights violations. In what would be known as the Maidan Uprising, protesters gathered in Kyiv's Independence Square. Over the next months the protests expanded into what would be known as the Revolution of Dignity. Fierce fighting occurred with frequent clashes between protesters and police. More than 100 Ukrainians died.

A memorial to victims of the Maidan Uprising

On February 21, 2014, Yanukovych signed an agreement with members of the Ukrainian Parliament. The agreement created an interim government, reformed the constitution, and called for early elections. The next day, the parliament voted to remove him from office. Yanukovych said the vote was illegal. He asked the Russian government for help. The Russian government did not recognize the new Ukrainian government and considered the ousting of Yanukovych to be a coup. Two days later, Yanukovych left Ukraine and fled to Russia.

During the Revolution of Dignity, there was destruction in the streets of Kyiv.

After annexing Crimea, the Russians built the Crimean Bridge across the Kerch Strait. The bridge links Russia and Crimea and is the longest bridge in Europe.

CHAPTER FOUR

RUSSO-UKRAINIAN WAR

Protests continued across Ukraine, with those supporting Yanukovych against those who wanted change. Russia took advantage of the chaos. On March 1, 2014, the Russian parliament approved a request from President Putin to send troops into Ukraine. Russia began moving forces into the Ukrainian oblast of Crimea, a peninsula on the Black Sea.

In the following days, Russian forces took over Crimea's communication and transportation systems. They took over the Crimean Parliament and restricted access to the peninsula. On March 16, Crimeans went to the polls to vote on whether to stay in Ukraine or be annexed by Russia. More than 95 percent of the votes cast supported annexation. Two days later, Russia annexed Crimea.

In April, the Donetsk and Luhansk oblasts, together known as the Donbas, declared independence from Ukraine. Pro-Russian separatists took control of government buildings and declared the Donetsk People's Republic and Luhansk People's Republic. They demanded a vote to declare independence from Ukraine and to join Russia.

The two republics held referendums on May 11, 2014. Both voted in favor of independence from Ukraine. The republics were supported by Russian forces. However, Ukraine did not recognize their independence. It sent military forces to end the uprising and to evict the Russian forces from the Donbas. When Petro Poroshenko was elected Ukraine's new president on May 25, he declared his first trip would be to the Donbas.

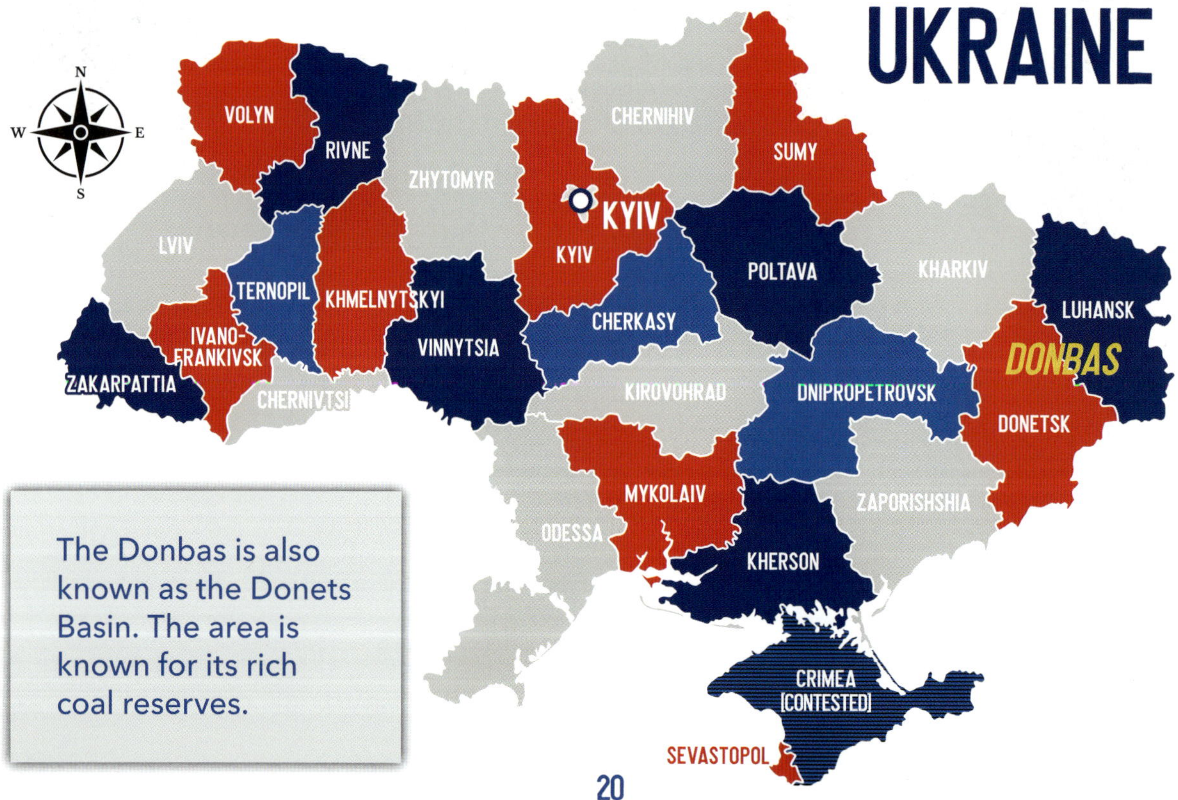

The Donbas is also known as the Donets Basin. The area is known for its rich coal reserves.

Citizens in Donetsk celebrate independence from Ukraine on May 18, 2014.

Several attempts were made at a cease-fire, but they failed. Finally, on September 5, representatives from Russia, Ukraine, the Donetsk People's Republic and the Luhansk People's Republic, and the Organization for Security and Co-operation in Europe signed the Minsk Protocol. This agreement had many goals, including a cease-fire. But still the fighting continued.

A man in Donetsk salvages food from an abandoned military site in February 2015.

On February 7, 2015, a new agreement was signed. The Minsk II agreement included a cease-fire, the removal of heavy artillery and foreign forces from the area, a release of prisoners, and a reform of Ukraine's constitution to decentralize power. This agreement also failed, and the fighting would continue for years. By the end of 2021, the conflict had claimed more than 14,000 lives.

On February 21, 2022, Russian president Vladimir Putin formally recognized the Donetsk People's Republic and the Luhansk People's Republic as independent states. This was followed with recognition by Cuba, Venezuela, Syria, and Nicaragua. Russia signed mutual assistance treaties and agreed to provide military assistance to the new countries.

That same day, Putin gave a televised address. In his talk, Putin acknowledged Russia and Ukraine's shared history and culture. He noted that from 1991 to 2013, Ukraine had benefitted from $250 billion in preferential trade with Russia. He accused Ukraine's government of failing to uphold financial agreements made after the collapse of the USSR. He declared that Ukraine's government was corrupt and served the country's oligarchs, not its people.

Since the separation of Donetsk and Luhansk from Ukraine in 2014, there had been repeated military conflict in the Donbas. Putin said towns and villages were shelled by the Ukrainian Army almost every day, killing civilians including women, children, and the elderly. On February 23, the Donetsk and Luhansk People's Republics formally asked Putin to send military forces to help them defend against these attacks.

President Putin with Luhansk People's Republic leader Leonid Pasechnik *(left),* and Donetsk People's Republic leader Denis Pushilin *(center).*

President Vladimir Putin prepares to address his nation from Moscow on February 24, 2022.

CHAPTER FIVE

SPECIAL MILITARY OPERATION

On February 24, 2022, Putin gave a speech to the nation. In it, he claimed that for eight years, the Russians had been working to settle the situation in the Donbas peacefully. He said forces that staged a coup against Ukraine's elected government in 2014 had abandoned the path of peaceful settlement. He said it was impossible to tolerate the atrocities inflicted on those who live there and that this was the main force behind recognizing Donetsk and Luhansk as independent states.

He criticized the actions of the US at the end of the Cold War. He said that the country did not respect the needs of others in the changes that took place. There had been an opportunity to remake the world to the benefit of all countries, but that was not the path the US

ARTICLE 51

Article 51 in Chapter VII of the UN Charter allows a member country to defend itself against an attack before Security Council approval. Typically, UN countries agree to follow Security Council decisions. On February 25, 2022, eleven of the 15 Security Council members voted for a resolution against "Russia's aggression." China, India, and the United Arab Emirates abstained. That month's council president, from Russia, vetoed the resolution.

had chosen. He continued by pointing out acts of what he called US military aggression including the wars in Serbia, Iraq, Libya, and Syria.

Putin also took issue with NATO and its expansion. When the USSR collapsed and the Cold War ended, the Warsaw Pact had dissolved. NATO, however, had not. At the time, United States secretary of state James Baker gave assurances to Russian president Mikhail Gorbachev that NATO would not expand eastward. However, since those assurances, fourteen countries had joined the Alliance, including Estonia and Latvia, which share borders with Russia.

Ukraine joining NATO is unacceptable, Putin said. He said it was Russia's historical land and that Russia would be threatened with NATO's armed forces and weapons systems in Ukraine. He accused NATO of supporting far-right nationalists and neo-Nazis in Ukraine and asserted that they would undoubtedly attack Crimea as they had the Donbas. He went on to say that while facing the permanent threat of NATO's presence in Ukraine, Russia could not exist.

In accordance with Article 51 (Chapter VII) of the UN Charter, the permission of Russia's Federation Council, and mutual assistance treaties with the Donetsk and Luhansk People's Republics, Putin had made the decision to carry out a special military operation. The goal of the special military operation was not to occupy Ukrainian territory, Putin said. It was to defend Russia from those who had taken Ukraine hostage.

Ukrainian president Volodymyr Zelenskyy prepares to address his nation after Russia's recognition of the Luhansk and Donetsk People's Republics.

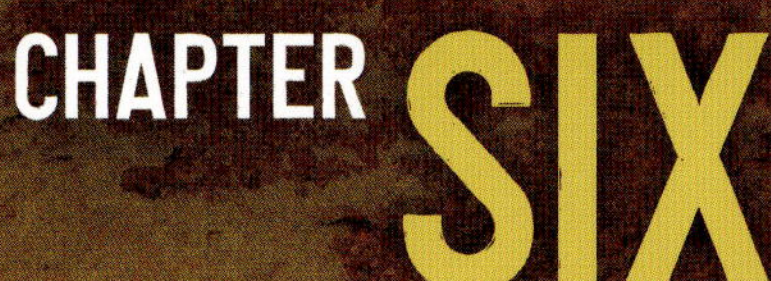

CHAPTER SIX

RUSSIAN INVASION

Soon after the conclusion of Putin's speech, explosions rocked Ukraine. Not only were there bombings in Donetsk and Luhansk but also in the cities of Kyiv, Kharkiv, and Odesa. Russian forces moved into Ukraine, crossing Ukraine's border with Belarus in the north, landing in the eastern port cities of Odesa and Mariupol, and moving in from the Crimean Peninsula. Ukrainian forces repelled Russian troops in the Luhansk, Sumy, Kharkiv, and Chernihiv oblasts.

Ukraine's president, Volodymyr Zelenskyy, had been elected on April 21, 2019. One of his campaign promises had been to end the war in the Donbas. During that year, he negotiated with the governments of the Donetsk and Luhansk People's Republics and with Putin.

Zelenskyy and the breakaway republics agreed to a cease-fire in July of 2020. But as was the case since 2014, the fighting did not end.

Now that the Russians had invaded, Zelenskyy acted quickly to restore order and keep Ukrainians safe. He declared martial law on February 24 and severed diplomatic ties with Russia. He also made independent news organizations illegal to protect Ukraine and its citizens against Russian disinformation. "Don't panic," he told Ukrainians. "We are strong. We are ready for everything. We will defeat everyone. Because we are Ukraine."

The Russians continued their offensive, seizing the Hostomel Airport near Kyiv and launching a second wave of bombing attacks on Kyiv, Odesa, Kharkiv, and Lviv. Later that evening, a fierce battle ensued near the Chernobyl nuclear power plant. When the fighting ended, the Russian forces had gained control of the site.

Ukraine needed a major military response to defend itself against Russia's aggression. To bolster Ukraine's military capacity, shortly before midnight, Zelenskyy signed a general mobilization decree and also forbade all Ukrainian men between 18 and 60 years of age from leaving the country.

Police in Moscow detain a Russian man who was protesting the invasion.

On February 25, Russian forces bombed Kyiv with ballistic missiles. Russians entered Kyiv from the north and attempted to assassinate government officials. President Zelenskyy was one of their targets. To defend the city, Ukraine's government distributed firearms to the citizens and deployed the military reserve force.

The Ukrainian forces prevented a rapid Russian advance. While Russia had launched a massive bombing campaign, it had failed to conquer any large cities. Ukraine's command structure was still in place and its airspace was still in use by both Russian and Ukrainian aircraft. Against this backdrop, both Zelenskyy and Putin indicated a willingness to talk.

The first round of peace talks was held on February 28, 2022, near Ukraine's border with Belarus. Ukraine's goals were an immediate cease-fire and full withdrawal of Russian troops from Ukraine. However, when the talks ended, no agreements had been made. The fighting continued.

Representatives for Russia and Ukraine met in Gomel, Belarus, for the first round of talks.

On February 24, European Commission president Ursula von der Leyen held a press conference on the invasion. The following day, she announced financial, energy, and technological sanctions against Russia.

CHAPTER SEVEN

ECONOMIC ESCALATION

The reaction of the international community was swift. Several nations as well as international corporations enacted sanctions against Russia. The goal was to disrupt Russia's economy. This would limit funding for the Russian military and cause hardship for the Russian people. "Putin is the aggressor," said US president Joe Biden. "Putin chose this war, and now he and his country will bear the consequences."

The consequences were extreme. The European Commission (EC), the United Kingdom (UK), the US, and Canada moved to remove Russian banks from the SWIFT system. Japan, South Korea, and Switzerland would later join this sanction. The European Union (EU), US, UK, and Japan kept Russia's central bank from using its assets to work around sanctions. Visa and Mastercard blocked Russia from access to their networks.

International companies such as Coca-Cola, Apple, McDonald's, and Nike stopped doing business in Russia. Automakers including General Motors, Volkswagen, and Mercedes-Benz stopped selling vehicles there. Microsoft and Samsung suspended sales of their products in Russia.

One sanction that had significant impact was stopping the Nord Stream 2 pipeline project. The pipeline is part of a system of natural gas delivery pipelines that run under the Baltic Sea from Russia to Germany. The Nord Stream 2 pipeline would have doubled the capacity to deliver Russian natural gas to Europe. The US banned imports of Russian products, and the UK announced it would phase out Russian oil imports by the end of 2022.

SWIFT

The Society for Worldwide Interbank Financial Telecommunication (SWIFT) is a secure messaging network through which international payments are sent. It allows countries to make safe business transactions with one another. When Russia's banks were disconnected from SWIFT, they became unable to send or receive secure international payments.

These were the harshest sanctions ever imposed on a nation. Russia quickly acted to counter these measures. The nations that had imposed the sanctions were declared to be "unfriendly." On March 31, Putin announced that Russia would stop natural gas exports to unfriendly countries unless they submitted payment in rubles. The EU imports almost half of its natural gas from Russia. Russia would not accept US dollars or euros as payment.

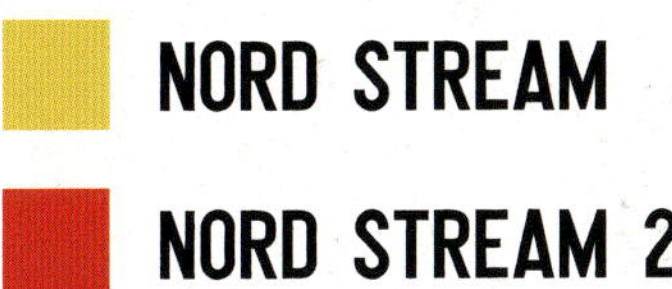

Nord Stream 2 began in 2011 and was completed in 2021. It had not yet begun service when German chancellor Olaf Scholz suspended certification of the project on February 22, 2022.

Russia had other leverage against the unfriendly nations. Russia and Ukraine are responsible for one-third of global wheat production. Many countries import most of their wheat from the two warring nations. The war had destroyed ports on the Black Sea. Cargo ships had been sunk, making shipping companies' insurance costs increase. This resulted in disrupted grain exports from both Russia and Ukraine, and in turn food crises in Africa and the Middle East.

Russia moved to use limited grain exports to its advantage against sanctions. Russian security official Dmitry Medvedev said, "It so happened that the food security of many countries depends on our supplies. It turns out that our food is our quiet weapon. Quiet

but ominous. We will supply food and crops only to our friends. We will sell both for rubles and for their national currency in agreed proportions."

Russia's targeting of the global food supply went further. While its major exports are oil and gas, Russia is also the world's largest exporter of fertilizer. In early March, the country recommended that its fertilizer companies suspend exports. The resulting surge in global fertilizer prices put a strain on the world's food producers. It also caused inflation in food prices, which caused civil unrest in some counties. The economic warfare was having worldwide impact. But the human suffering went beyond the cost of food.

On March 10, people from the cities of Bucha and Irpin evacuate along a humanitarian corridor.

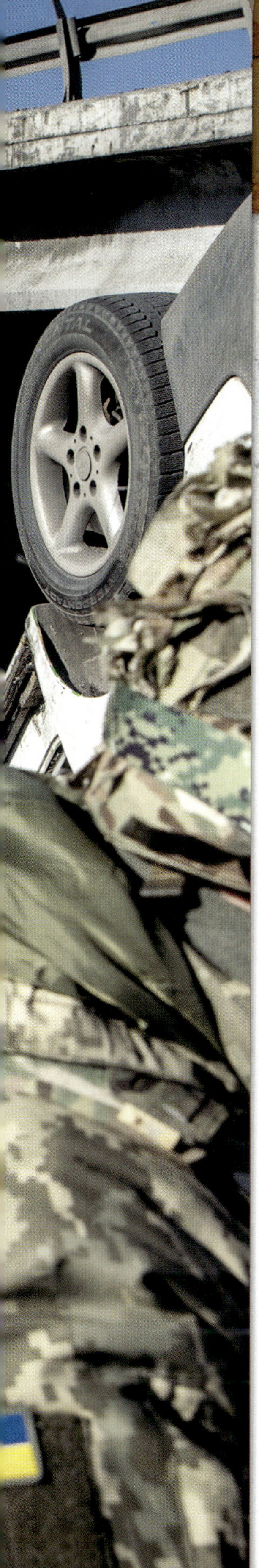

CHAPTER EIGHT

HUMANITARIAN CRISIS

A second round of peace talks was held on March 3. Zelenskyy asked to negotiate with Putin directly. The Russian president did not agree. While the talks ended again with no agreement, both Russia and Ukraine said they would open humanitarian corridors so civilians could evacuate. Two days earlier, the UN had appealed for $1.7 billion to serve the needs of Ukrainian refugees.

The funds were sorely needed. There was a mass exodus from Ukraine. Refugees poured into neighboring countries. Poland welcomed the highest number of refugees, the peak coming on March 6 at more than 140,000. That day was also the peak for Romania, with more than 36,000 refugees entering from Ukraine and Moldova. As the war progressed, other nations extended aid to refugees. The Czech Republic would issue more than 350,000 emergency visas, and Germany would welcome more than 700,000 Ukrainians.

The UN estimated nine out of ten refugees were women and children. Ukrainian men were banned from leaving the country. Some refugees needed specialized care. Others were elderly and disabled. Officials were concerned about the safety of vulnerable refugees such as LGBTQ individuals. All refugees needed safe shelter, food, water, medicine, and hygiene.

The EU quickly provided medical equipment, oxygen, masks, and gowns. Medical teams worked to evaluate people and move the very ill to medical facilities. Refugees were given food and shelter and social welfare benefits.

An elderly woman is evacuated from Kramatorsk on a special ambulance.

While staying in a bomb shelter, a Ukrainian woman cares for a child she does not know so his parents can get some rest.

Ukrainian refugees in Poland register with the United Nations High Commissioner for Refugees to obtain cash benefits.

The EU also activated for the first time in its history the Temporary Protection Directive. This allowed Ukrainian refugees the right to live and work in their host countries for up to three years. It also allowed refugees a pathway to citizenship in their host countries.

The UK offered visas to Ukrainians who had family living there. It also allowed British people to let a Ukrainian individual or family live with them for six months. Refugees could live and work in the UK for up to three years and receive health care, welfare benefits, and education.

The US announced it would provide $1 billion in humanitarian assistance, $320 million in human rights funding, and accept 100,000 refugees. It also supported Children and Family Protection and Support Hubs. At these locations, refugees could access legal aid, mental health support, food, and hygiene areas.

Since February 24, more than 6.5 million people had fled
Ukraine. More than 7 million had been displaced from their homes
but had stayed in the country. World nations had responded with an
outpouring of aid to assist refugees in becoming established and
integrated in their host countries, perhaps permanently. Meanwhile,
the situation in Ukraine was not improving.

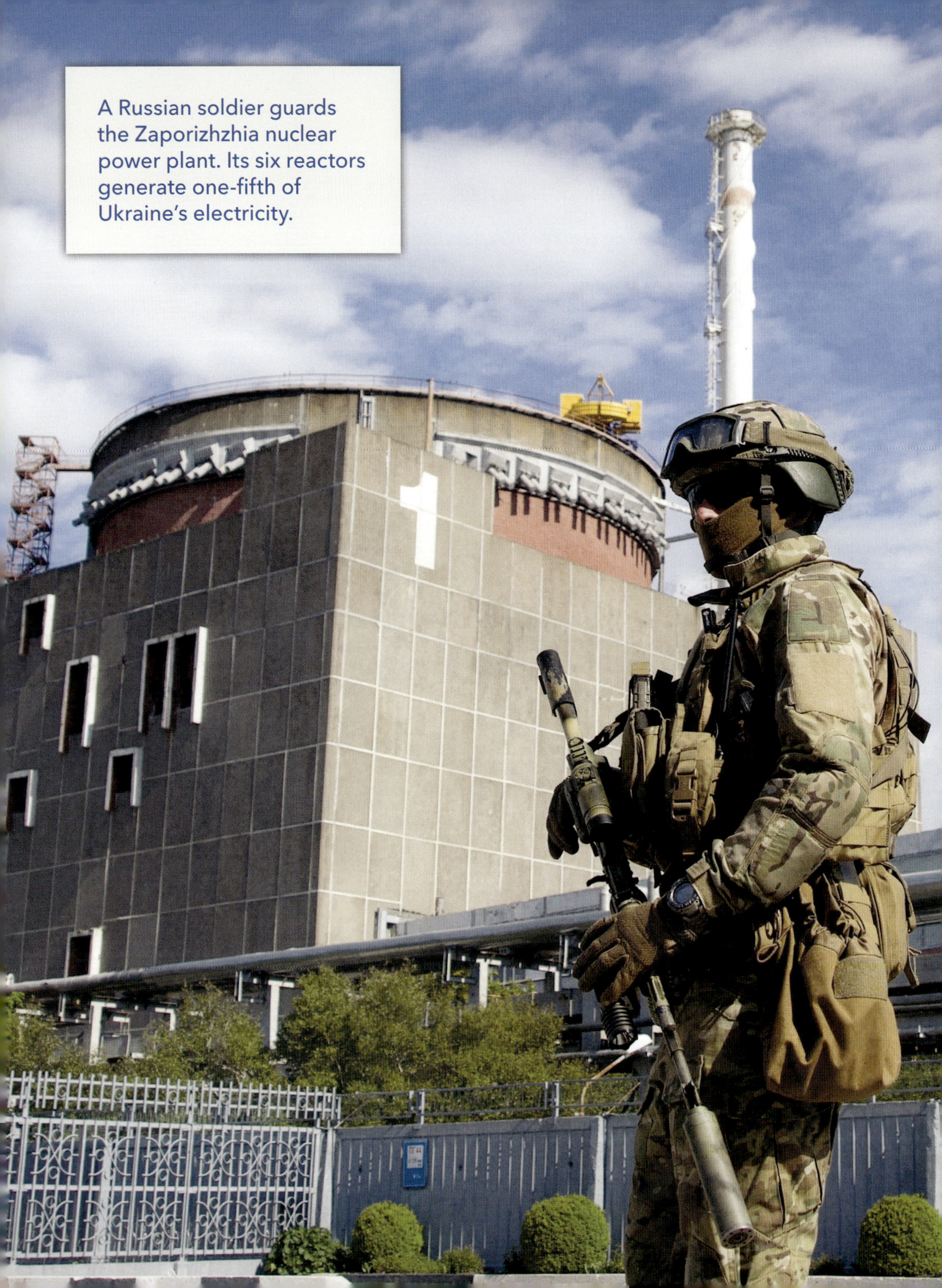

A Russian soldier guards the Zaporizhzhia nuclear power plant. Its six reactors generate one-fifth of Ukraine's electricity.

CHAPTER NINE

NO END IN SIGHT

On March 4, Russian forces had captured the Zaporizhzhia nuclear power plant, Europe's largest. Russian forces continued to advance. Three days later they captured the cities of Vasylivka, Tokmak, and Polohy.

But Ukraine's military continued to regain ground and retook Mykolaiv International Airport and Chuhuiv. Amid the continued destruction, Turkey hosted a meeting between foreign ministers Dmytro Kuleba and Sergey Lavrov on March 10. Once more, the two sides were not able to reach any agreements.

To this point, Russia had focused on securing areas in eastern Ukraine. But on March 11, the Russians turned their attention to western Ukraine, attacking and destroying Lutsk Air Base and a military base at Ivano-Frankivsk

International Airport. The next day, the Vasylkiv Air Base was destroyed.

Meanwhile, peace talks had resumed, this time virtually. Russian negotiators wanted a neutral, demilitarized Ukraine. Ukraine rejected this and proposed neutrality while keeping its armed forces for defensive purposes. Again, the two sides failed to come to an agreement.

United States president Joe Biden traveled to Warsaw, Poland, on March 23 to meet with Ukrainian officials. In a speech, he supported Ukraine's war efforts. "A dictator, bent on rebuilding an empire, will never erase the people's love for liberty," he said. "Ukraine will never be a victory for Russia, for free people refuse to live in a world of hopelessness and darkness."

On March 29, Ukrainian and Russian negotiators again met for peace talks. The in-person meeting in Istanbul, Turkey, included proposals that Ukraine become a neutral country, that the status of Crimea be negotiated, and that Russia would withdraw from Ukraine to preinvasion positions. Russian officials announced a reduction in military activity surrounding Kyiv. Yet once again, the talks failed to stop the fighting.

By early April, Ukrainian forces had pushed the Russians out of Kyiv. Russian forces were also retreating from other positions. After Russian forces left the city of Bucha, Ukrainian authorities accused them of executing and mutilating civilians there. They provided images showing more than 1,000 bodies that were found after the

Russians withdrew, including 31 children. Russian officials denied responsibility. The Russian Ministry of Defense called the claims "a provocation."

The city of Bucha after the retreat of the Russian forces

On April 7, Russian foreign minister Sergey Lavrov rejected the Ukrainian proposals delivered at the peace talks in Istanbul. He said the Russian delegation would submit a counter proposal. That day, the UN voted 93 to 24 to suspend Russia from the Human Rights Council because of alleged atrocities. The EC also announced additional sanctions against Russia. They included banning Russian coal and other fossil fuel imports beginning in August, denying Russia access to EU ports, and banning exports of jet fuel and electronics.

Accusations of Russian war crimes continued on April 8, when a train station in Kramatorsk was hit by a Russian rocket. At least 57 people died. Photographs quickly circulated that showed bodies lying on blood-stained pavement amid scattered suitcases. Again, the Russians denied the accusations. They claimed that the type of missile used in the attack was used by Ukrainian forces.

On April 13, an explosion occurred on the Russian ship *Moskva*. The ship was in the Black Sea to assist in the invasion. Ukrainians claimed to have hit the vessel with two anti-ship missiles. The Russians claimed that a fire onboard had caused munitions to explode. Although the cause of the damage was unclear, the Russians began to tow the vessel back to port. But the ship sank before reaching its destination. Later it was revealed that Ukraine used US intelligence to sink the *Moskva*.

Five days later, Russia launched a hypersonic missile for the first time to destroy a weapons depot near Ukraine's border with Romania. Hypersonic missiles can travel at 10 times the speed of sound and can elude air defense systems. After this display of power, Foreign Minister Lavrov announced that phase one of the special military operation was complete.

The *Moskva* entered service in 1983.

This handout from the
Russian Defence Ministry
shows the launch of the
RS-28 Sarmat, also known
as Satan II. President
Putin announced that it
would be in service by
the end of 2022.

CHAPTER TEN

A NEW PHASE

Russia began the second phase of its special military operation on April 20 by testing a new nuclear-capable intercontinental ballistic missile. In a statement the Russian Defense Ministry said, "Sarmat is the most powerful missile with the biggest hitting range in the world. It will significantly strengthen the combat power of the Russian strategic nuclear armed forces." Russian officials said that with four of these missiles, the East and West Coasts of the US could be destroyed.

Ukrainian and Russian forces had been struggling for control of the port city Mariupol. On April 17, Ukrainian foreign minister Dmytro Kuleba said, "The situation in Mariupol is both dire and heartbreaking. The city doesn't exist anymore." Then on April 21, Russian defense minister Sergei Shoigu announced, "Mariupol has been liberated."

But there were Ukrainian forces, including members of the Azov Battalion, occupying Metallurgical Combine Azovstal. This iron-and-steel producing complex was built by the USSR and began production in 1933. A series of tunnels under the structure protected workers from a potential nuclear strike during the Cold War.

Putin decided not to storm the plant to capture the embedded forces. "We should always think, in this case especially, about saving the lives and health of our soldiers and officers. There is no need to climb into these catacombs." Instead, he chose a different military tactic: siege. "Block off this industrial area so that not even a fly can escape," he told Shoigu. Putin's plan worked. In less than a month, the soldiers hiding in the plant's tunnels would surrender.

The war's destruction was taking a toll on Ukraine. On April 21, Zelenskyy told the World Bank that Ukraine needed $7 billion a month in financial assistance to make up for losses from the war. He said the Russian blockade of Black Sea ports had disrupted grain exports. This affected not only Ukraine's economy but also global food security.

The next day, Russian major general Rustam Minnekayev announced the goals of the second phase of the special military operation. They were to fully occupy Donbas and southern Ukraine, establish a land bridge to Crimea, and gain access to Transnistria, a breakaway republic in the country of Moldova. These goals were in contrast to what Putin stated in his February speech. Putin threatened to strike any nation who interfered with the plan at "lightning speed."

To show support for Ukraine and to pledge additional financial aid for military operations, Secretary of State Anthony Blinken and Secretary of Defense Lloyd Austin flew into Poland and then traveled to Ukraine on April 23 to visit with Zelenskyy. Blinken was confident in Ukraine's victory. "In terms of Russia's war aims, Russia has already failed, and Ukraine has already succeeded," he said.

Mariupol sustained heavy damage as the Ukrainians and Russians fought for control of the city.

President Biden signs the Ukraine Democracy Defense Lend-Lease Act as Senator Ben Cardin and Ukrainian-born representative Victoria Spartz look on.

CHAPTER ELEVEN

SLAVA UKRAINI

On April 28, the US reiterated its support for Ukraine when the House of Representatives approved the Ukraine Democracy Defense Lend-Lease Act. This would allow the US to send weapons to Ukraine and other Eastern European countries. These countries promised to pay for these materials at a later date. The bill had already passed in the Senate. On May 9, President Biden signed the bill into law.

Biden followed the Lend-Lease Act with a request to Congress for an additional $33 billion in aid for Ukraine. The funds would provide military equipment, food, water, and shelter, as well as assist other nations who welcomed Ukrainian refugees. "The cost of this fight is not cheap, but caving to aggression is going to be more costly if we allow it to happen.

We either back Ukrainian people as they defend their country, or we stand by as the Russians continue their atrocities in Ukraine," the president said. The House of Representatives approved an increased aid package of $40 billion. It passed in the Senate on May 19 and was signed by the president two days later.

As the war in Ukraine neared its fourth month, there was speculation that it could go on for years. But world support was backing Ukraine against the Russian invaders. In April, Speaker of the House of Representatives Nancy Pelosi had traveled with other representatives to Kyiv to meet with President Zelenskyy. The group said in a statement, "Our delegation traveled to Kyiv to send an unmistakable and resounding message to the entire world: America stands firmly with Ukraine."

During the meeting with Zelenskyy, Pelosi echoed the support of the American people. "We believe that we are visiting you to say thank you for your fight for freedom. We are on a frontier of freedom and your fight is a fight for everyone," Pelosi said. "Our commitment is to be there for you until the fight is done."

Speaker Pelosi and
President Zelenskyy in Kyiv

TIMELINE OF THE WAR IN UKRAINE

The Russian invasion of Ukraine in February 2022 was the largest military action in Europe since World War II. The effects of the crisis, from destruction in Ukraine to food shortages and inflation around the world, were widespread.

FEBRUARY 21, 2022

Russian president Vladimir Putin recognizes the Ukrainian regions of Luhansk and Donetsk as independent states.

FEBRUARY 25

Russian forces bomb Kyiv with ballistic missiles and attempt to assassinate government officials, including Zelenskyy.

FEBRUARY 24

Russia invades Ukraine. Ukrainian president Volodymyr Zelenskyy declares martial law and severs ties with Russia.

FEBRUARY 28

The first round of peace talks is held near Ukraine's border with Belarus. No agreements are made.

APRIL 2022

Russian forces retreat from Kyiv and other locations, including Bucha. Images from Bucha show more than 1,000 bodies that were found after the Russians withdrew.

APRIL 8

A train station in Kramatorsk is hit by a rocket. At least 57 people die.

MARCH 31

In response to strict sanctions from the US and other nations, Putin announces that Russia would stop natural gas exports to "unfriendly countries."

APRIL 7

Russian foreign minister Sergey Lavrov rejects the Ukrainian proposals from the peace talks in Istanbul. He says the Russian delegation would submit a counter proposal.

APRIL 13

An explosion occurs on the Russian ship *Moskva*. The vessel sinks before it can be towed back to port.

Slava Ukraini is the Ukrainian national salute. In English, it means "Glory to Ukraine."

MARCH 3, 2022

A second round of peace talks end with no agreement, but Russia and Ukraine say they will open humanitarian corridors.

MARCH 6

Poland welcomes more than 140,000 refugees.

MARCH 4

Russia captures the Zaporizhzhia nuclear power plant.

MARCH 29

Another round of peace talks take place in Istanbul, Turkey. Again, the talks fail to stop the fighting.

APRIL 18

Russia launches a hypersonic missile to destroy a weapons depot near Ukraine's border with Romania. Lavrov announces that phase one of the special military operation is complete.

MAY 9, 2022

US president Joe Biden signs the Ukraine Democracy Defense Lend-Lease Act. The bill allows the US to send weapons to Ukraine.

APRIL 20

Russia begins the second phase of its special military operation by testing a new ballistic missile. A few days later, the second phase's goals are announced, including occupying Donbas and southern Ukraine.

MAY 21

Biden signs a $40 billion aid package for Ukraine.

GLOSSARY

annex – to take land and add it to a nation.

assassinate – to murder a very important person, usually for political reasons.

asset – something of value owned by a person, business, or government.

atrocity – an especially terrible act or thing.

ballistic missile – a weapon guided upward in a steeply curving path before falling freely.

blockade – the cutting off of an area by soldiers or ships.

catacombs – winding underground tunnels used to bury the dead.

confiscate – to take away by one's authority.

coup – a sudden, violent overthrow of a government by a small group.

democracy – a governmental system in which the people vote on how to run their country.

deploy – to spread out and organize in a battle formation.

dictator – a ruler with complete control who often governs cruelly.

exodus – a large moving away of people, animals, or things.

industrialization – a widespread change from an agricultural to an industrial society.

insurance – a contract that pays people money if an important thing like a house or car is wrecked. People pay money to keep the contract.

interim – standing in until something permanent is formed.

leverage – resources or situations used to gain power over others.

martial law – military rule imposed on the general population during a war or other emergency.

munitions – explosives, weapons, or ammunition, such as bullets.

nuclear triad – a military force consisting of land-, sea-, and air-launched nuclear weapons.

oblast – a political and administrative division within a country.

oligarch – one of the rulers in an oligarchy, or group of wealthy people using their money for governmental influence.

referendum – a direct vote by the people on a public matter.

sanctions – actions by several nations against another nation to force it to obey an international law.

satellite – a manufactured object that orbits Earth. It relays scientific information back to Earth.

separatist – an advocate of separating from a larger group.

shell – to throw explosives on or at something.

visa – a stamp on a passport that allows a person to enter and leave a certain country.

To learn more about the war in Ukraine, please visit **abdobooklinks.com** or scan this QR code. These links are routinely monitored and updated to provide the most current information available.

INDEX